FOR
THE CHILDREN
OF
~~████~~ ~~████~~ ~~████~~
Enjoy Reading!
FROM:
The Auroraland Auto
Restorers Club
2002

Under the Quilt of Night

by Deborah Hopkinson

illustrated by James E. Ransome

An Anne Schwartz Book
ATHENEUM BOOKS FOR YOUNG READERS
NEW YORK   LONDON   TORONTO   SYDNEY   SINGAPORE

RUNNING

I'm young
but my legs are strong.
I can run.

I run so fast,
I lead the way;
the ones I love race right behind.
Pounding dirt and grass,
jumping rocks and roots,
my feet make drumbeats
on the path.

I'm running far
away from the farm
where the master worked us,
hoeing and picking,
mending and sewing
till my hands got raw.

Now he wants to track me,
catch me,
chase me till my breath is gone,
fence me in to be a slave again.

But I'll make my steps
quick whispers in the dark.
I'll run where he won't find me,
under the quilt of night.

A river!
We search long
to find the little boat
hidden in the reeds.
Is it safe to go over?
The water's deep and fast.
But we cross
without a sound,
like the moon coming up over my shoulder
to float across the sky.

WAITING

Runaways like us
must hide in daylight.
So come morning
we crouch in the bushes
till night.

It's hot.
Sweat dribbles down my neck.
Thorns rake my arms and legs.
In the still afternoon,
mosquitoes whine and tease
just like the overseer's children did.

All I can do is wait
for the cover of darkness.
Oh, if only
I could dance into the open
and sing so loud
the stars would hear
and hurry out to guide our way!

WATCHING

We run and hide, run and hide.
My cuts sting, my bites itch.
I'm hungry all the time.
One day at dusk
we make our way to a patch of woods
at the edge of a town.
There are more houses here,
people, roads—
danger.

The others rest,
while I keep watch for a sign
from the Underground Railroad—
the friends who will help us get free.

Whoee whoee whoee,
an owl trills softly.
I stop my breath to listen.
Is it really an owl or
the railroad's secret code,
a sign that a friend is near?
No, there he is—just a small, fat bird,
with round, yellow moons for eyes.

I try to be an owl myself,

but my eyes hurt with watching.

Then I see a woman walk

through her yard

wearing a plain dress.

On her arm she carries a quilt to air.

She hangs it over the fence,

then looks to the woods,

just once.

I stare with all my might.

I know what to look for:

in most quilts, center squares are red

for home and hearth.

But these centers are a dark,

deep blue.

This house hides runaways!

I'm brave enough to go forward first.

When at last the stars are up,

I pull the darkness around me

and run through long, wet grass.

My foot trembles

on the wooden step,

and my knock is shivery and quick —

like the beating of my heart.

"Who's there?" comes a voice.

I swallow hard before I give

the password.

What if I am wrong?

But I trust the quilt, so I say,

"The friend of a friend."

HIDING

A man and woman let us in.
They give us clean clothes,
hot stew and biscuits,
sweet cherry pie.

We talk in whispers
so we won't wake their little boy,
already tucked in bed.
Their daughter, just my age,
lets me hold her kitten.
We follow her lantern
up narrow stairs to a secret room.
"Sleep now.
Tonight we'll keep watch,"
she says.

I lie awake wondering

about others who have hidden here.

I won't ever know their names.

But I find a message,

a rough carved place

in the wood under my mat.

I make my fingers into eyes

to explore it.

Just before I fall asleep

I see it is a star.

TRAVELING

"Wake up! Hurry!
Your master and his men
are close behind!"
Our friend whisks us through the
last folds of night
and hides us deep in his wagon.
The cold boards make me shiver.
Straw pricks my skin like needles.

We go north
across a bridge, under trees,
a zigzag of here and there.
We can't turn back —
we would be beaten, sold away,
our chances gone for good.
We must go on or die.
I hang on tight.
Fear is so real, it lies here beside me.
The wagon rattles, horses clomp.
Suddenly I tremble.
Voices!
We're caught.

"We're looking for runaways.
What's in your wagon?"
barks a voice.
"Eggs, sacks of grain, vegetables
to sell at morning market," says our
driver, smooth as honey.
"Search me if you like. I'm no friend
of the slave."

I keep still
as a rock
though it feels
like my heart will split.
But the searchers are fooled
and at last they gallop off.

Our friend laughs
and cracks the reins.
He calls to his horses:
"Giddyup, Hope and Liberty!"
And the wagon rolls on.

SINGING

Birds wake,
a rooster calls.
I listen to night
softly falling away.

We stop at a little church
deep in a piney wood.
I pick the straw from my hair
and rub my stiff, cramped legs.

Our friend takes a stick

and draws a map in the dirt

of the road we'll take to Canada.

"These good folks will carry you on," he says.

"You're almost to freedom now."

Over the trees the sun comes up.

The dark pines glow like gold.

Freedom!

I take a deep breath

and when I let go

my voice flies up in a song.

My own song

of running in sunshine

and dancing through fields.

I'll jump every fence in my way.

A NOTE ABOUT THE STORY

Under the Quilt of Night is an imagined journey. It is a fictitious story inspired by the Underground Railroad, and it mixes fact and folklore. The Underground Railroad, of course, was not actually underground. Nor was it a railroad. It was a secret network of people who helped others to escape slavery. It was most active in the 1850s, in the years just before the Civil War.

Just as we don't learn the name of the girl who tells this story, we don't know the names of most who escaped on the Underground Railroad. Activities took place in secret and weren't written down. Those fleeing slavery faced incredible danger and hardships. The free blacks and whites who helped them also faced risks.

Many stories have grown up around quilts and the Underground Railroad. Some think quilts included hidden meanings or were hung to mark safe houses, while others believe these stories are simply folklore.

We do know that fugitives were hidden in many ways, sometimes in secret rooms or tunnels, other times in wagons with false bottoms, or simply under straw in the back of carts. We also know from songs like "Follow the Drinking Gourd" that enslaved people used the North Star to help them locate north, where Canada and freedom lay. In this story, the girl finds a star someone has carved in the floor as a hopeful sign of freedom.

When I was a fourth grader, the Underground Railroad was mentioned in just a few lines in our history textbook. Today many books and Internet sites have information about this part of our history. In communities people are working together to remember family stories and to find and preserve Underground Railroad routes and houses. But some of our past may always be hidden from us.

—Deborah Hopkinson

For Deborah Wiles, Jane Kurtz,
and James Ransome, with heartfelt
thanks and admiration
—D. H.

To Bob and Jean Cunningham—
thanks for everything
—J. R.

Acknowledgments

Special thanks to Jacqueline L. Tobin and Raymond G. Dobard, Ph.D., authors of *Hidden in Plain View,*
A Secret Story of Quilts and the Underground Railroad; and Cuesta Benberry, three people who generously
gave of their time to answer questions.

Atheneum Books for Young Readers
An imprint of Simon & Schuster Children's Publishing Division
1230 Avenue of the Americas
New York, New York 10020

Text copyright © 2001 by Deborah Hopkinson
Illustrations copyright © 2001 by James E. Ransome

Book design by Ann Bobco
The text of this book is set in Adobe Minion MM.
The illustrations are rendered in oil paint.

Printed in Hong Kong
10 9 8 7 6 5 4 3 2 1

Library of Congress Cataloging-in-Publication Data
Hopkinson, Deborah.
Under the quilt of night / by Deborah Hopkinson ; illustrated by James Ransome. — 1st ed.
p. cm.
"An Anne Schwartz Book."
Summary: A young girl flees from the farm where she has been worked as a slave and uses the
Underground Railroad to escape to freedom in the north.
ISBN 0-689-82227-8
1. Underground railroad—Juvenile Fiction. [1. Underground railroad—Fiction. 2. Fugitive
slaves—Fiction. 3. Slavery—Fiction. 4. Afro-Americans—Fiction.] I. Ransome, James, ill.
II. Title.
PZ7.H778125Un 2000
[Fic]—dc21
98-31290